P9-DHM-345

It's Christmas!

CollinsPublishersSanFrancisco
A Division of HarperCollins*Publishers*

Lighten Up, It's Christmas

Lighten Up, It's Christmas

Santa Goes To The Dogs

Santa Goes To The Dogs

Christmas
Comes To The
Desert

A Packaged Goods Incorporated Book
First published 1996 by Collins Publishers San Francisco
1160 Battery Street, San Francisco, CA 94111-1213
http://www.harpercollins.com
Conceived and produced by Packaged Goods Incorporated
276 Fifth Avenue, New York, NY 10001
A Quarto Company

Library of Congress Cataloging-in-Publication Data
Schulz, Charles M.
[Peanuts. Selections]
It's Christmas! / by Schulz.
p.   cm.
"A Packaged Goods Incorporated Book"—T.p. verso.
ISBN 0-00-225029-2
I. Title
PN6728.P4S3225   1996
741.5'973—dc20   96-15704
                        CIP

Printed in Hong Kong

1 3 5 7 9 10 8 6 4 2